The
Power
Of Inspire

Journey of Extra Ordinaries

ANKAN SARKAR

Preface

'The power of inspire' is a twenty-first century creation which consists of short stories about families, failure, societal and many other everyday life matters. The stories would open the eyes of the readers and give them a message about the purpose of living which is lost in this generation.

This book also asks the readers to make a promise that they would never do anything which would hurt someone from both outside and inside. Love is expressed from the heart, not words. However, anger is expressed from the words, not from the heart.

Contents:

1. Genius for No One.   4

2. Early Success.   20

3. Behind Achievements.   46

4. A Hero from Nowhere.   76

Genius For No One

When someone talks about Rohan, "He is a perfect option", "A good one for our company", "Only we want him", "He is the best", and of course he was one of the best students in campus. He was excellent in academics and was a champion debater.

In sports he was like the backbone of his team. He was the best cricket player in his school and even in campus and college. His charm had attracted many people which had also benefited him in getting a good job from his campus.

But for one thing he had been hated from others and even from himself after few years

Which led him to a fall from a high place, not physically but mentally.

Was it overconfidence, love or any other reason. Was it because of any failed promises. Let's find out his journey to find out the main reason which led such a great man from success to failure.

During the monsoon months of July, a bright happiness was born in an upper middle class house from which the falling of the raindrops could be heard along with the tears joy from a couple who have just now become parents.

You have been wondering why not in a hospital, because the new father was an achieved doctor who had assistants in his house for emergency help.

The father arrived and just a second later and found his newly born son, sleeping in a baby bed.

"Thank you so much Radha for this most valuable and happy moment. I would do my best for him in my entire life" said Venkatesh from the depth of his heart.

His wife, Radha, was sleeping for almost half an hour before he arrived. Venkatesh went out to bring some useful goods. The news had reached the entire neighborhood and he received congrats from almost everyone.

When he came back, he found his wife awake and his son, still sleeping, in her lap. Venkatesh came near her and took the baby in his hands.

He said in a low voice, "You will rise up so high and your name will be Rohan."

His wife was happy with the given name and she smiled at her husband with gloomy eyes. The whole household even including the assistants were very happy.

This was the beginning of Rohan's life which started in a desirable manner.

Thus, years passed on happily with Rohan getting everything on a single demand. At the age of four, he started attending school.

His first day in school was a good one. He entered his classroom to find many children of almost his age were sitting on benches, writing on notebooks and enjoying with their friends.

His teacher was a sweet lady whom everyone liked and listened.

Rohan made many friends on his first day only and he spent time with everyone and helped them.

But no one knew that on his first day of school, Rohan would learn an important life lesson.

What was that lesson which someone could learn at that age? Well, learning has no limit and it does not look any age or something.

During the lunch hour, Rohan's friends were going outside for having a hand wash but Rohan didn't want to go. He thought that someone would eat his lunch. One of his classmates told him that he would look at his tiffin, he may go. Rohan believed him blindly and went. He came back and found his lunch box is gone. He then cried for the whole day and none of his friends offered him food. He had a ten rupees note and he bought something to eat with that.

That day he learnt a lesson that he should not blindly believe anyone and even his friends at the cost of something valuable.

The readers may feel that Rohan should not accuse his friends, but this life lesson is from a four-year old child point of view.

No one is born hating someone. The hatred is created by the society which can even lead someone to become a criminal. But don't worry, Rohan would never do something like that.

'Criminals are not born, they are made.'

Years passed like an express train. Rohan has started attending secondary school. In a very young age, he was surrounded by competitors in academics. But this didn't effect Rohan at all.

He had a very special ability. Rise up but not alone, with everyone. He was good in studies and had a keen interest on commerce. His rising ability attracted everyone including his school principal who once said, "Rohan is the leader of growth."

That sentence inspired him much more and he did even more hard work than before. He was driven by a desire to work and excel.

Even in sports, he was a great leader. He was the captain of his school cricket team. But during the finals of the inter-school tournament, his team lost the match.

The players insulted him a lot and told him that he should focus on studies rather than sports.

Rohan had a big heartbreak. He had worked

hard for the tournament, planned very well but could not make it at last. He was very upset that day. Everyone blamed him for the defeat.

The readers should tell what a captain can do if players don't play well. That's not the captain's fault.

Rohan wasn't happy. All his work went in vain. He thought that he was the best but it led to his downfall. But, he didn't give up. He didn't give up his ability to rise with others and continued to earn victories in life.

But that match stayed in his mind forever. Would this effect his mind later. You have to find it out.

Even good people are effected from this kind of incidents. Let's see what Rohan has got.

Again years passed and story of Rohan continues as he topped in his school in the senior secondary examinations.

He got admission in a business college in Delhi where for four years he studied the subject.

During these five years, many incidents happened with him. He was the most successful student in the whole campus. He also continued his cricket career in that campus and won many tournaments with his team. He got offers from clubs but he was not interested. His main focus was on studies.

During the first year, Rohan thought that he should also use his old ability in the college also. But that didn't work.

He took his friends to the top but himself left

behind alone. All of his friends celebrated the victory of first year exams but Rohan was inside his room, sitting and thinking deeply.

At that time, his phone rang. It was Priya. Who is this new character? Was it his girlfriend? Wow! Sorry to say but 'no'. Priya was his friend, his study hour friend.

Rohan picked up the phone but stayed silent.

From the other side she said in a calm voice, "Hello, Rohan." There was no reply.

She raised her voice, "Rohan! Hello!".

"Hello, Priya, How are you" said Rohan when he was back in his senses?

"I am good but it seems that Rohan is not in his

prime form."

"Priya you know the reason then why are you insulting me like that, calling my name."

Priya waited for a moment and said with a professional tone, "Rohan, I know that you are a good student from the starting but in college you can't rely on the same strategies you used in school. College is a high level thing and you should change your strategies. I bet that you will be successful."

She took a pause and continued, "Do you understand what I have said just now?"

Rohan finally found what mistake he did. He responded her, "Yes, thank you for the advice. Bye for now."

"Bye" said Priya and cut the call.

Rohan thought that changing strategies was to change is ability. Rise up but alone, not with others.

But everyone will hate him if he does that. "So what? No one thought about me then why should I think of others. They did not do anything for me." With this thought he decided to prepare for the next year.

This was not easy for his friends. Rohan had stopped talking with them and did all his work alone. He only shared everything with Priya and not anyone else.

Priya was also a good student. In the first year she also scored well and was close be achieve rank first.

In the second year, it was as expected from

Rohan before the examination.

He scored almost perfect and achieved rank first but at the cost of his ability. That year he completely lost hi ability.

Rohan's friends didn't score well this time which proved that he has lost his ability.

Who was the cause for this, 'Priya'? Not at all. It was because of his other friends and Rohan himself.

Rohan was happy with the result but his friends didn't talk to him. Only Priya congratulated him that day.

Rohan thought that he would continue this next year also. And he did it next year.

But the next year, he was dissatisfied with the result announced. Priya scored the first rank. He was second. He couldn't stand that.

Priya called him several times but he didn't show any interest. He thought that Priya knew his strategy and so, he decided to change it one more time.

But this time, the strategy was very offensive.

My readers please never use this kind of strategy in any time of your life. This may result in something very bad.

Rohan's new strategy was rise up alone but stop your competitors even if they are your best friend.

This was the dangerous strategy he applied.

He studied a lot in the final year but also he distracted his friends and other competitors. He also distracted Priya which resulted in the break of his friendship.

He thought in himself that he would do this only in the final year and later again he would gain his ability. He risked his character for his career.

This resulted in Rohan scoring rank first but all his competitors scoring less and even worst. He also got a job package of sixty lakhs per annum.

When he returned home after scoring his degree, he was welcomed by his childhood friends of neighborhood.

His parents were very happy and they decided to have a party in the evening when all his parents had invited their colleagues.

After the party, Rohan decided to come back to his original character. He called his college friends but no one picked up.

Not even Priya picked up her phone. And why should they? Rohan was the reason for their downfall. He had no right to call them.

Rohan found out everything. He was upset and that reflected in his eyes. His parents saw him upset and asked him what had happened.

With a dissatisfied voice, he said "I have got everything in my life. A good job, rank and other things. But I lost my most valuable people from which I learned how to be a human."

Early Success

The sound of the crowd could be heard from several kilometers away from the auditorium. Why was a crowd gathered in the auditorium? Is there any function? It was more than something like a function.

The crowd was waiting for one of the most successful young singers in West Bengal, Nayan Dey. He was only seventeen-year old but he sang like a professional singer.

Nayan had already won two reality shows in West Bengal and also conducted several shows. He has won hearts of any people at a young age.

After few minutes, the crowd went wild in joy as the greatest young singer arrived on the stage.

The sound of the guitar and the keyboard reached several houses in the neighborhood.

After that Nayan sang a song with his famous voice had reached many ears in the entire state.

After the ending ceremony, the crowd started chatting with themselves.

"He will be a greatest singer in the future"
"His future is very bright"
"Nayan is an inspirable icon for the youngsters".

In the same day, during the night time Nayan received calls from his friends who told him that he was amazing and cool.

Nayan thanked them for their complements and they exchanged some thoughts with each other.

Nayan's parents were very happy thinking that he has made his future at a very young age and there is no need for them to think much about him.

His father proudly says about him in front of there friends and relatives.

But no one had ever thought that this would be the last performance of Nayan in his life.

What could have happened? How can a very young talented person fall so fast?

Well, the answer for these questions are hidden in his past. His past had several incidents which created him and it may even destroy him.

West Bengal is a state where music has it's own importance. This land has contributed many songs and singers in the Indian film industry.

Many famous singers such as Kumar Sanu, Subir Sen, Shreya Ghoshal, Arijit Singh and much more personalities were born in West Bengal.

It was the month of October. Dilip was returning from his office. He was in a hurry.

The reason was not something trouble but the opposite. He had received a call from the nearby hospital that he had become a father of a newly born son.

At the hospital his wife, named Renuka was waiting for her husband to see him surprised.

Within a few minutes, Dilip arrived.

Tears fell from his eyes which can be felt by him only for a newly father. He still couldn't believe his eyes.

His small son was sleeping beside Renuka. He picked him up and started gazing him with his eyes, still wet from tears.

His wife said in a calm voice, "I have selected a very good name for our son. I know you will also like it and even our son." "What name you have selected" asked Dilip, excitedly?

"Nayan", replied Renuka with a smile.

Dilip agreed with it, "Yes, a perfect name for our son." He went wild with happiness and started dancing inside the room.

It was their day. They enjoyed it very much.

As years passed, Nayan grew up. He was a very smart and intelligent child. He even got good marks in his lower classes.

But he was not at all interested in studies. He was very much interested in music, especially singing.

From a very young age he had been listening to songs of many famous singers. He had even attended many shows and concerts of his favorite singers. His interest was increasing day by day which later turned to be a life goal.

With the decision of becoming a singer, his life was completely changed. He never attended any classes for singing or music. His parents said that he had a natural ability.

With more practice, he was improving himself.

Daily he learned new tones and songs. He also developed his own technique of singing and his own voice.

He was very much dedicated towards music. He dreamed of meeting his favorite singers and to sing with them.

But for achieving or becoming something, it requires hard work more than something else. Even your passion and talent is not enough.

Nayan also thought that he would have to wrok hard for his success. But his expectations were fulfilled at a very early age.

He went to Kolkata to give auditions for a reality show which was going to held for 5 months in West Bengal. At that time, he was only twelve years old, a sixth class student.

When he arrived at the given place, he was surprised. So many children of almost his age were standing on large queue.

He also made his way on it. He was thinking in his mind, "My dream is going to be true, but so many competitors. Will I get what I want? Maybe Maa Durga is with me. I will succeed. Just give your best. Come on! I can do it."

After almost of two hours standing in the long line, finally his chance came.

He was nervous, thinking that four people had already made their way to the top Fourteen. Very few spots were left. He have to make it.

The entry gate to the stage were few steps from him. His heart beat was increasing. He took a deep breath and went on the stage.

He saw the judges were sitting in front of him just like in televisions. He was standing at the centre of the stage. All eyes were on him. He saw his father sitting behind the judges.

Obviously, this kind of situation can make nervous to anyone, but for Nayan, any kind of situation couldn't affect his singing.

Without any delay, he took a deep breath and started his song. He sang one of his favorite songs of Arijit Singh 'Sanam Re' with his most developed voice.

He sang with proper notes and tunes which a singer requires to make everyone lost in it.

He had a very mature voice at a young age. The judges were really lost in his voice. The audience was cheering. His father was feeling proud.

The high notes of that song was very difficult, but he sang them fluently like a professional.

His mature voice was also heard by the four other participants who had already made their entry to top fourteen. They were also shocked by that voice which was like an elder.

Nayan went on like this maintaining every single note. He finally finished his last note and when he opened his eyes, the judges were giving him a standing ovation.

He saw his father praising him. Dilip was overcome with happiness. He went towards the stage and hugged his son.

The judges praised Nayan a lot and they also asked him few questions about his extraordinary fluency. He was eager to tell everything.

He told them everything about himself that he has learned singing from himself only and no teachings. He has also learned few instruments by himself.

The judges understood that this was his natural ability and they didn't want to miss such talent. So, without wasting time, they directly selected him in the top fourteen.

Nayan's happiness knew no bounds. He jumped on the stage with excitement. He shouted with joy, "Finally! I am heading towards my dream."

Nayan didn't work much hard but still he got his dream. But this is not to be taken so lightly. Becoming a singer is not that much easy for someone. With the selection in the show, Nayan's life changed completely.

Nayan didn't do any extreme practice but still his voice was maintained well mature.

Nayan was doing more good than before every time and this further became regular for him.

He thought that no one can beat him in this profession and he overtook himself as the best contender in the show.

He became overconfident. Even the judges could find in him about his over confidence.

They also thought that the over confidence would led him to fall, but the total opposite thing happened which made them shocked.

Nayan was qualified for the finals of the show with the help of votes given by audience. He was a popular young icon for the youth.

Within few months, Nayan's growth was unimaginable for anyone. He became famous in the whole state of West Bengal.

The finals were upcoming in next week. Everyone was working hard and were trying to make their way to the trophy.

Nayan was also practicing but he was not very much serious for the finals. He knew that he has got the highest votes and had a very good chance of winning the trophy and the big amount.

Even the judges knew that Nayan was on a very good position. But they didn't want Nayan to win the show.

From a few weeks, Nayan was very over confident. But he never did any mistake in his singing, which even boosted his conviction.

The judges didn't wanted someone arrogant to be a winner even if he is a child.

That's why they planned a challenge during the end of the announcement of the winner. That challenge would change the level of the game. It would be the greatest surprise ever for the first time in that show. What could be the challenge?

The time has now finally come. The grand finale of the biggest blockbuster show in West Bengal. Five contenders, but only one winner.

Everyone was waiting for the starting ceremony. The show was broadcasting live for the first time. The whole neighborhood was gathered in front a big screen to watch Nayan lifting the trophy.

But the big surprise was waiting for everyone.

The show started with the inspiring voice of the young talents which were going to represent themselves in the film industry later.

The whole finale went smooth like a butter and between them some traces of salts. Nayan gave one of his best performances during the final which boosted him up.

When all performances ended everyone thought that the winner would be announced now.

But the judges at last gave the big surprise which was even more big for Nayan.

The surprise was bonus fifty, which meant that one last performance by all the finalists and one of them who will receive extra fifty votes from this contest. The audience was thrilled by this since it could even change the result.

Even the participants were surprised and few also thought that this was the best opportunity to beat others and capture the trophy.

The most surprising among them was Nayan. He had been the best throughout the whole show but the judges didn't like him.

He also thought that the judges had made this thing intentionally. But if he wants to win then he should earn those bonus fifty points.

All participants were good and this would be a tough part. Even the judges are not with Nayan which makes it impossible.

But Nayan didn't give up. He decided that even if the judges were not with him and the winner is to be declared by them, he will force them through his voice and they will award him.

Nayan thought about a song. He thought in himself, "Today I will sing the best song and my most favorite one which would make even the judges lost."

The song he selected was the first song he sang when he started singing, *"Besabriyaan"*.

He quickly revised the lyrics and also heard the original voice one more time before he could perform it.

"One last time and it is mine. Come on Nayan! You can do it. Lets do it!"

The five finalists were up on the stage. Nayan's turn was last, that means he has got a right opportunity to make his voice impactful.

The final battle started between the singers.

The audience were silent, listening to each and every notes of the finalists. Even the judges were observing them.

The judges have already decided in themselves that except Nayan, anyone can be the winner.

They listened to each and every voice carefully. Each participant was giving their best performance in the entire history.

Among the judges, they had already decided that the second singer would be awarded bonus points. But Nayan's performance was left and he had already decided to make it.

The four performances were over. Now it was Nayan's turn. He looked into the audience. His parents were sitting there. He closed his eyes and started his performance with a bright smile.

The first line of the song, just captured the judges' attention. The song was from the film, 'MS Dhoni: The Untold Story'.

It was a motivational song even one of the best of that time. The song in Nayan's extra ordinary voice was reflecting his past and his journey.

The judges could feel his voice in their hearts. The voice, which didn't show any arrogance or any indiscipline.

Nayan had closed his eyes. His full focus was on the song, catching even the smallest parts and notes which make the deepest impact.

Dilip was listening to his son. He has never thought that his son would be something like this. He was feeling very proud. His wife's eyes were in tears.

Nayan was about to finish his song. The other participants were also lost in his voice. That day his voice was sending a message to his competitors and to his audience.

The judges were forced to finally change their decision. They have decided to award the bonus fifty to Nayan. They haven't thought that they would ever do this.

Nayan finally finished his song. When he opened his eyes, the scene was something which would make someone proud.

The entire public stood up and clapped for him. He saw his parents doing the same. Even the judges stood up and cheered for him.

This was the victory for Nayan. He did what he wanted to do and he has now achieved it.

It was now time to announce the winner of bonus fifty contest.

The judges stood up and without wasting time, they shouted, "None other than, Nayan."

The crowd roared with excitement. Nayan lifted his hand and the whole place shivered as if an earthquake has come.

He was awarded the bonus fifty points. Now no one could stop him from lifting the trophy.

Everyone knew that it was Nayan who's going to make it. His parents were very happy. They only wanted him to achieve something in life and he has done it.

It was time to announce the winner. The crowd was waiting for the closing ceremony.

The director and manager of the show entered on the stage to award the trophy and announce the winner.

Nayan was holding his breath for the upcoming excitement among the crowd.

"The winner, of the fifth season, of WB Rock stars is Nayan."

And the rest was history. Nayan achieved something very big in life. At a very young age he has expressed himself in the world as one of the greatest young singers.

The newspapers' headlines read, "Rock star Nayan has won the WB Rock stars reality show of West Bengal."

The whole West Bengal discussed about this.

When Nayan came back to his town, he was welcomed by the whole neighborhood.

A warrior has returned after defeating everyone and leading victory on the trophy.

The readers might think that how he got everything at a small age? Well, this is not everything he received.

In the next year, he was invited on another reality show, 'WB Champions'.

He participated in that show and even won that. No one has ever thought that someone could win two reality shows in consecutive years and at a young age.

Every body thought that he was a genius guy and was born for singing.

But the readers should always remember that even legends are not always consistent.

And Nayan was just a teenager. During the starting of the story he had conducted a show in an auditorium.

I had mentioned that it was his last performance. The readers now would come to know why that was his last performance.

Nayan had already won two shows in West Bengal. But he was not satisfied. He thought of getting a tough competition.

For that he decided to participate in the greatest show ever in India from which many singers have risen up.

He was thinking about, 'Indian Idol'.

He was sixteen years old and he could participate.

He went to Mumbai with his father. He saw a long queue which reminded him about his past when he had entered on the stage for the first time.

He thought that this time also, he would make it. He gave the auditions and impressed the judges. He was even selected for the grand auditions.

But during the grand auditions, he was rejected as the judges mentioned that they couldn't take someone with so arrogance in his voice.

This sentence became viral especially in West Bengal. The impact of this was something Nayan haven't imagined in his life.

Nayan's popularity slowly came down and almost lost. He conducted shows but no one came to visit him. He cried for audience but didn't get anything.

As a result, he had to sing in restaurants and hotels for his living. In the same year his father died of Heart attack.

All responsibility was on him now and he didn't get any time for comeback. His friends tried to help him but couldn't do anything.

The rest of life went in sorrows. Someone who was titled as a future legend was now struggling to secure his future.

Early success could bring everything you want but it would also lead you to an early failure from which recovery is the toughest.

Behind Achievements

Rajesh was a very responsible family person. Even if he belonged to a lower middle class family, he managed to handle everything.

From the childhood onwards he started to help his mother and father. He loved helping others even at the cost of his own losses.

Maintaining this attitude, he became a very responsible person. Even in office hours, he maintained this behavior and was awarded the employee of the year.

Rajesh was good, but not the best of his kind.

In the world of this generation, you can only become best by winning the race and surpassing your competitors.

If you try to help others, you would only be called as 'good'.

This was the reason why Rajesh was good but not the best. Then who was the best?

When Rajesh was in his college, he had participated in the elections. But his opponent was the most successful candidate in the college history.

His name was Manav. He was even the college topper in his first and second year.

Both Rajesh and Manav were in the same year. Rajesh joined elections for the first time in second year but Manav had been participating from the first year onwards.

This makes him more vulnerable to win the election.

Rajesh gave his best but still couldn't win. He found out that Manav forced his friends and other students. Even he gave them some money also.

Manav even got the highest job package from the college. On the other hand, Rajesh got only a package of six lakhs per annum.

This difference made Manav the best and Rajesh only a good person.

But Rajesh never let it affect him. He didn't desire to be the best at the cost of his values. His character was more important than money.

After few months of winning the employee of the year, Rajesh was married to one of his old classmates, he liked during school time.

Her name was Reena. Rajesh liked her not only for her external beauty but also for her inner soul and her character.

When he found that he would be married to her, his happiness knew no bounds.

Even Reena was happy. She wanted someone with not much money but with a responsibility.

She knew Rajesh from school time and knew all about her. That's why without even wasting a single minute, she agreed for the proposal.

They both married each other on a very good occasion of Thursday night.

Within few years, they had a daughter. They named her 'Neeti' which means an act of living a good and responsible life.

Rajesh's family was a lower middle class one. They decided to spend money wisely. They planned that they would seek interest of her daughter first and then would prepare.

But within few years they had one more child, a son this time. They named him 'Nipurn'. Neeti was only five years old at that time.

Rajesh was now at a very big problem. Managing two children for a middle class family was very difficult.

Reena once talked to him about this matter, "Let it be as it is going. If we get any problem we will see later. Nothing to worry about it now."

Thus, years passed and both Neeti and Nipurn studied in a nearby school. But the fees was very high and to afford it, Their father had to work overtime also.

Then a very important decision came in front of Rajesh. This was a very expensive decision which would decide what should be the future of their children.

Neeti has just completed her tenth boards and she got an average percentage. Nipurn was on class sixth but he was very good at academics.

But Rajesh couldn't afford any more money for their education. He could only allow any one of his children.

But this would be unjust to force someone to leave their studies. He was at a huge tension.

Reena saw her husband in trouble. She came near to him and said in a low voice, "I know the reason of your problem. You have been taking this responsibility from the starting onwards. Now you should take a wise decision."

Rajesh understood what she wanted to say. He said to her, "I know Reena but what should I do? I don't want to stop my children's education."

"Speak slowly, they will hear it", whispered Reena.

Reena doesn't want her children to listen what they were talking about.

Nipurn was outside the house playing with his friends but Neeti was doing his work inside. She heard everything her father was talking about.

She was writing something in her notebook but her hand stopped, her pen fell down.

She heard the serious matter of her parents. She came outside on the balcony and started thinking about the matter.

"They are talking about financial issues. I think someone has to quit the school but who should do it.?"

She saw her brother from the balcony. Everyone was congratulating him for scoring rank one in his class. He was very happy at that time.

Neeti said to herself, "Yes, I will do this. I don't want my brother to be called as uneducated. He deserves to get what he has done it. As an elder, I will sacrifice for him and he will also remember me for this act. Someone has to do it and most probably the elder one. I love my brother very much and I can do anything for him."

Without wasting a single minute, she went inside the room where her parents were discussing. She knocked the door.

"I want to tell you something very important. Please listen to me very carefully", said Neeti.

Rajesh wondered what she wanted to tell. She has never talked so seriously like that in her entire life. He said, " What is the matter, why you look so serious? You have never been like that before."

"I know what you are wondering about but it is really very important" said Neeti.

"Then tell me, how can I help you" asked her father.

Neeti started her concern, "I have made this decision by thinking a lot. I have decided to leave school. I want my brother to be well educated. My education doesn't matter a lot. That's why I have decided to quit. You don't have to invest much on me. Use it for my brother instead. He is even better than me in studies. He has the right to be educated."

Rajesh was in a shock. Never in his life he had ever thought that her daughter will do something like this.

Rajesh tried his best to convince her to continue school but she insisted on herself.

She told her father that he should not waste money on her and invest it in right decisions.

She even told that when his brother would earn, he will resolve all their problems.

After so much of discussion between the group, Rajesh finally decided to allow her daughter to leave school.

But he wasn't happy with that decision. He had never thought in his life that his own child will sacrifice for his another child. He never wanted someone to stop education but Neeti did it all for his brother.

The readers should tell if her decision was right or not? If not, then what else they should do to continue their education.

I know that you would say about loan. But the history of taking loans among the lower middle class family was worst.

Even Rajesh had once thought about taking a loan but her wife told her that he had already taken insurance and other things so he might get a loan but he would not be able to repay it back.

Moreover, he is also working overtime and he can't increase his salary more than that.

This was the reason for not taking a loan which resulted in her daughter leaving school.

Neeti again came to the balcony. She saw her brother smiling. She said in a very calm voice, "Now you will always smile. You don't have to compromise. Go ahead and achieve."

Neeti remembered something she forgot to tell her parents. She quickly went inside the room.

Her father was still in a serious mood. She also said in a serious tone, "Please don't tell Nipurn that I have left school for him, he would not understand anything. Tell him that I got low marks and didn't get admission further."

Rajesh did as her daughter said. Now if she had decided, let it be going like that.

When Nipurn returned home, he got to know everything which happened in his absence. He asked his sister why she did that. Neeti told her that she didn't get admission due to low marks and now she would not attend school anymore. Her journey for education would end here and now she would stay at home.

Neeti also told him that if he didn't study well in higher classes then he would also not get admission in school.

Nipurn understood everything. He thought that if he failed then he couldn't show his face to his friends anymore. He then determined that he would never let anyone to defeat him.

Day and night, Nipurn worked hard. He didn't wanted to be like her sister who failed in the exams, as he was told by her. But he didn't know that due to her sister's sacrifice, he was able to study in a good environment.

Nipurn's hard work didn't go waste. Every time he topped in his class and honors spread in front of him. He was interested in cracking JEE and join IIT in the future.

Thus, years passed very fast like a bullet train and it was the era of Nipurn.

He topped in his school in higher secondary. In the same year before his 12th boards, he gave the JEE mains exam.

When result was announced, it was only Nipurn and Nipurn! No one had ever thought that he would get AIR 99. This rank was the biggest achievement in his life.

His whole family celebrated the victory with joy. Nipurn was very happy that day. But more than him, or the happiest one among them was Neeti.

She thought in herself that her sacrifice was worth it and his brother will succeed.

After few months Nipurn gave the JEE advanced exam. His heart beat was increasing during the result day. His sister was even more worried.

But the result announced was worth it. He was selected in the IIT Delhi. Even he got his favorite subject.

His sister was very happy. She herself faced all the tags of uneducated. She cried inside her soul but never showed it in front of his family.

She was the original person behind her brother's achievements.

She even came with her brother till Delhi to give him company. When her brother went inside the dream building, tears flowed down her eyes.

But she didn't show her tears to her brother. She didn't want him to feel stressed because of this.

Her brother went inside the dream building and would return after four years. Neeti has now just to spend four years and then her sacrifice would be proven by her brother.

But these four years would not be easy as she has to spend it without her brother.

That's why she decided to do something in these four years. The work she decided didn't require much education. She had studied till tenth standard and it was good enough for her to go on.

What was the work she decided to do? What was the purpose of that work?

The purpose was something very important and very special for Nipurn. The main result of the work would be known at the last.

Rajesh had collected the fees by working day and night. He even announced that he would only take retirement after completing his son's education.

Responsibility can turn even an indolent person to the most hard working one.

Rajesh from the starting was a responsible person and it took his entire life struggling for his family members.

Now it was the final stage for him where he would know if his hard work would pay off or it would go waste. Hope for good.

Thus years passed again and again. You know that time never stops.

The family was waiting for there result. And finally, finally they have received what they have hoped for.

The 'chirag' of their house was back after completing B-tech. The moment was something to be remembered for years.

Nipurn has even got a high package job of sixty lakhs per annum. The family now shouldn't struggle for money anymore.

Every member was happy but the most happiest one among them was again Neeti. Now she could proudly say that she is the brother of and IIt-ian.

Her friends taunted her a lot and even called her "Uneducated". But she faced everything from the front.

She suffered a lot for her brother getting a job and now she was satisfied that her sacrifice didn't go in vain.

The celebrations were not over yet. Neeti's friends were standing outside the house. She saw them from the balcony and immediately went downstairs.

One of her friends said to her, "We are really sorry for what we did in the past. We shouldn't had left you alone. That was the time when we should support you but we taunted you and made you feel discomfort. We apologize from the depth of our hearts."

Neeti didn't understand what to say. She didn't wanted her friends to feel guilty and at the same time she wanted them to get lost of her sight.

But she was not the kind of person who break relationships only for a small matter.

She said, "It's okay. I am glad you realized your mistake but it took so many years. Still I have doubts about you all. What can you do?"

"You do not need to doubt us anymore. Wait near your house tomorrow morning. We have planned something for you" said one of her friends.

Neeti noticed her brother was calling her. She said to her friends, "Guys I have to go. Let's meet you all tomorrow, bye for now."

The whole night of Rajesh's family went on party and celebrations. After some time, all the guests went back.

Nipurn was standing alone on the rooftop, lost in his own thoughts. Neeti saw him and stood beside him.

"Oh! You scared me" muttered Nipurn.

Neeti started laughing and after some time, she said to him, "What are you going here alone, whose thoughts you are lost?"

"In my own thoughts only, who else is here?"

She again laughed and said, "Oh! Are you sure about that? I don't think so you are in your own world. I never saw you like that. Tell me."

After looking here and there and ensuring no one is watching them, Nipurn said in a low voice, "Actually, I am lost in someone special's thoughts. I know her since class 11th. She was my best friend. Apart from friendship, I started liking her."

Neeti was surprised. She started wondering how her brother cracked IIT. He asked, "What's her name? Tell me if I could help you."

"What can you help? You didn't even completed your education. If you went in front of her with me, she will reject me because of you. You have failed in your examinations. I don't want you to talk to her. Anyway, her name is Priya."

Neeti didn't like his behavior.

She didn't even like the words he told her. He called her uneducated. Yes, she was uneducated but for whom she did that, didn't know the truth.

She didn't tell anything and quickly went inside her room.

She saw her parents had already slept. She lied on the bed and started crying. Hiding her tears beneath the pillow. But even after trying she couldn't change her feelings for her brother.

She loved her brother very much, even more than her parents. But she had never thought that her brother would give her a treatment like this.

She desired to struggle not only for her brother but also for her family to maintain the required sum of money.

She didn't like her brother's attitude towards her. She thought that her brother has forgotten he was also a child before getting IIT.

She understood that arrogance has taken place in her brother's mind. Therefore, she decided to bring back her original brother.

The readers would think that I am only talking about brother and only brother. Don't worry, you will see in the end.

Neeti wanted him back to his old attitude but how could she do it? What is the method or the trick? Well it was simple, Nipurn should be made realized about what he had did.

And for that, Neeti had already done what she wanted to do. What was that?

Neeti wanted to meet the one whom Nipurn likes, Priya. Only Priya could make him realize his mistake.

Nevertheless, she didn't know anything about her. Not her address, mobile and even her face. How could she find someone unknown in a big city? It would be very difficult for her alone. Only Nipurn knows about her but he would never share the required information.

However, if she wanted to make her importance towards Nipurn, she had to find her at any cost.

For that, she thought of meeting one of his brother's friends. She could get everything and his friend must know about the girl Nipurn was talking about.

Raghav was a very close friend of Nipurn. He used to share everything with him which included even his personal thoughts and desires.

Neeti knew about Raghav since when his brother was a child. She decided to meet him.

When she met him, was shocked to hear his words. She immediately responded, "What! She died in an accident."

"Yes, Nipurn also knew about this. That's why he was not that much happy even after getting a good job" said Raghav with regret.

Neeti thanked him for the information. She was very upset for her brother. She wondered, "Nipurn didn't even tell me that she died this year. That's why he was looking changed that day."

Neeti was very upset. She thought that she could make him realize but his brain was affected by the accident.

Now she had only a last chance to bring back his brother. It was the hard work she did in those four years when Nipurn was in Delhi.

Her work could change Nipurn's life. It would definitely make him realize about his fault.

Neeti met her friends the next day. One of them was a business influencer. she told them everything about what had happened. Her friends decided to help her.

What was the idea or the work for which she used her four years of time. Was it something special? It was more than that.

In the next week there was a rush among the media to take an interview of a new writer who had published her first book. Her first book only had made a deep impact on the public.

The writer of that book was Neeti. She wrote about her sacrifice and her autobiography of her journey towards her brother's success.

Her story had inspired many young people and especially the younger brothers who had an elder sister.

She gave an interview and announced her story to the world. She told that her friends played a very important role in the publication.

Nipurn never thought in his life that he would become a brother of a author.

For two days he read the book. His eyes were filled up in tears. He finally realized his mistake.

He went to her sister, sat in front of him. He took her hand and said in a low voice, "I am sorry. I had always thought only negative thoughts about you. I even called you failure several times. However, I never thought that it was you because of which I am now a successful person. It was you behind achievements. Please forgive me although I do not deserve it."

Neeti felt she had received the victory. Tears flowed form her eyes same like her brother. She smiled and hugged her brother.

With that smile on her face and tears in her eyes, Neeti said in a low voice, "Don't do it again."

A Hero From Nowhere

From his childhood onwards, Arjun was a great fan of Japanese characters which included samurai or ninja. He used to love their fighting skills and especially their weapons.

He had seen in movies, anime and even read books of such characters. He even love the honors and the code of these warriors.

Due to these things, he didn't have any interest in studies and even sports.

This was the problem which his parents could never solve in his entire childhood.

However, the problem continued even after getting a good college for studying. He studied hard even after not having interest just for his parent's sake. "I do not want my parents to feel that they have wasted money on me" he thought in his mind.

But, Arjun's love for the warriors didn't vanish. He loved them and especially their katana. He thought and even desired that one day maybe he would buy a katana license.

Arjun now had to spent five years in an engineering college for completing his degree.

These five years would not be easy for him as there would be a huge problem and even a worst incident which was waiting for him. What was that incident?

In the first year of his college only, he got a bad news that his parents died in an accident. When the news reached Arjun, he was totally blind and broken.

His friends offered their condolences to him. They even told him that if he required any financial support, they are ready to help.

Although, Arjun's father has already paid the half fees for the time period, he has to ask for the remaining to his friends.

But he took it as a debt since he didn't want anybody to make him under someone.

This type of incident would make anybody cry for the whole life. Arjun was just a normal person. This was the biggest heart break for him.

Few months passed and Arjun tried to forget that incident but he couldn't. Though he managed to move up and to become a successful person.

However, who knows that something very strange and even something very surprising was waiting for him which would change his life.

(This never happens in real life, readers should go only with the story and just understand the moral.)

One night when Arjun was totally tired of the activities, he slept early. In his dream, he saw his father. He was totally shocked. His father said, "Arjun, I know you are struggling a lot. But it is for your good only. Today, I will give you a special power which you would love, but use it wisely and only for good deeds."

He shouted in his room and quickly woke up from his bed. His heart beat was running like a bullet train. He tried to calm himself and looked at the clock, 5:00 am.

He talked to himself, "What was that? Why did my father came to my dream. This never happened before. What was the purpose? He said that he would give me a special power."

Arjun didn't get what he had seen. He thought that this was just a silly thing, he was very tired yesterday and maybe he was thinking a lot about his parents. That's why this happened.

Therefore, without thinking much about his dream, He started preparing for the classes. However, the words of his father remained in his mind the whole day.

Arjun went to his classroom. He studied for the whole day and it went just like normal classes.

He decided to check the locker room once as he has forgotten something. He searched for his locker and he remembered that his few documents were inside that.

When he opened it he saw something very strange. It looked like a black shuriken. His old memories came back in front of him when he took it in his hand.

He thought who must have kept it there since it was not his own. He looked here and there to search for someone but in the while locker room, he was standing alone. He thought that someone might have gifted him, so he took it to his home along with the important documents.

Arjun came back to his hostel room. He didn't have any roommate since the other bed was not in a good condition.

However, he didn't knew that a surprise was waiting for him in his room which he had never thought of in his life.

When he opened the cupboard door for changing his clothes, he was surprised to see that his clothes were lying down inside and a mysterious black suit which looked like a ninja's armor was hanging there.

For a moment, he couldn't believe his eyes. He pinched himself as if to ensure he was not in a dream.

He asked himself, "What is this?"

He then at once remembered about his father coming into his dream. He said to himself, "That means it was for a purpose. My father wants me to do this and I will do it. This suit was my dream."

He took out the suit and found that there was a box behind it. He found that a space was given for a star shape object.

He then quickly noticed about the shuriken which he got from the locker room. He took it out and placed it, lo! It was unlocked.

When he opened the box, he found the dream weapons which he had seen in movies and read about it in books.

The main one among them was the katana.

The katana was about forty inches long of full size and it was covered with a thick-shiny black colored sheath. It was even decorated with ribbons and it's grip was made with a classical cloth.

Arjun took out the katana and saw it's sharp metal which was shining like a diamond. The cover above the grip was made with gold. Overall, it was for him only.

Inside the box, he also found two Kanto's (a secondary weapon of ninja's), few shuriken's and few kunai's.

He also found a letter in which it was written, "My son, this is your gift for not disobeying me. Use it for good deeds. You are now a hero of this city. Go ahead and don't worry about skills."

He found that he would not need to learn anything, his father had transferred him the skills of the warriors. He was very happy.

He quickly wore his suit, attached all the weapons and looked himself in a full size mirror.

He was looking like a ninja, wearing a mask and a cover on his head. His katana was attached behind his body, the kanto and other tools were kept hidden inside the suit and only he could access it.

He waited till midnight as he thought of visiting the streets at the darkest hours. He would also have to ensure that no body see him otherwise they would think him a thief.

The moon came out as the ninja went for.

He tried his first jump from one roof to another roof but he was scared. However, when he successfully made it, he never looked back or down.

He went on like the wind which never stops. His speed was five times the original one. He could even use his katana with a mastery skill.

He noticed that he could walk like a cat, without making a sound. When he saw patrolling cars of police, he hid himself and went along the roof lines.

He was enjoying his outdoor activities which were quite different from the normal ones. Even these are impossible for a normal one.

Once you wear the suit, the skills are inbuilt.

Arjun took a round of the city and came back home. He enjoyed the night very much while running on the roof tops. He could even jump from the top floor of a sky-scraper without any difficulty.

That night when he slept, his father again came to his dream. His father said, "Well done my boy. You have finally accepted my gift. But this is not only a gift, it is a responsibility which you have to take. From tomorrow onwards you are on a duty. And remember one most important thing, you have two lives, one with this suit and powers and the other is your normal. When you will die, you will be alive again but your powers will be lost and you will be a normal person again. So, be careful. From now I won't come to your dreams. This was the final time. Good luck." Saying this, his father disappeared and he again woke up early in the morning.

He went in front of the window from where he could see the sunrise. He said to himself in a calm voice, "I won't make your gift go waste. I promise that I will be responsible."

He got himself ready for the college and went on. When he entered the gate, he felt something very positive. He had never felt like that before.

When he entered his classroom, he could see his friends chatting something serious.

He joined them, "Hey Guys! What's the matter? Why you are looking so serious? Tell me."

One of his friends told him that he had seen some shadow sort of thing running yesterday night. He saw it on the roof tops of the buildings.

He even told that he had seen it last falling from a high building. When he went there for searching, he found nothing.

He was scared as he was alone so, without wasting any time, he left that place for his house.

None of his friends believe him and even Arjun acted like he slept very early due to tiredness. But he wondered how someone could see him as he was lightning fast and who remains awake in the midnight.

He asked his friend, "What were you doing in the streets at midnight. Are you doing something illegal?"

He rejected it and said that he was in a party and he had to go there, it had been necessary.

Arjun thought in his mind, "He never went to any party. Then what could be the reason for such a necessity? Something is wrong, I need to find out. I will follow him tonight."

During the end of the college hours, Arjun told his friends that he would be unable to join them for sports as he had very important work to do in his father's old office which was in that city only.

However, the original work was known to him only, a very important one.

He quickly went to his room, closed the door and opened the closet. He saw his suit, "Today I have my first job with you. Let's do it."

He wore the suit, the mask, assembled his weapons and was ready for the mission.

He waited till dark on the rooftop of his friend's house. His friend's name was Rahul Yadav. They both know each other from class 11th.

Many hours passed and when it was 11:00 pm, he saw his friend coming out. He lived alone in his house so, he can do anything there.

Arjun followed him till he found that Rahul was meeting some people who were looking like gangsters. He knew that something was wrong.

Rahul went with them in an under construction building. When Arjun saw it, he was surprised to watch the scene. The whole building was guarded by people carrying firearms. It was confirmed that they all were doing illegal things and also targeted Rahul for their expand.

Arjun thought in his mind, "This is the best time to charge. But wait, if I go straight to attack, their leader might run. I should go with stealth."

He then silently walked towards the guards. When he got an opportunity, he strike them down without anybody noticing him. He killed the two guards who were inside a car.

Then he saw someone smoking near the sewage pipe. He took out his kanto and silently sent him to hell.

He then went to the top floor with the help of his self-made grappling hook. He saw the leader of the group. He was a fat and tall person with a long rifle in one hand and a cigarette on the other. He saw his friend Rahul was begging in front of him and he was laughing.

Arjun became very angry. He threw a kunai towards the fat person and it struck his neck. Within seconds he died sitting on his sofa.

The guards surrounding him were horrified to see their boss lying dead. They became alert.

Nevertheless, the saw a shadow coming out from the stairs. Without considering the situation, the guards started firing at it but they found their guns empty and none of the bullets went on target.

Very soon, Arjun took out his katana and slashed each guard with the perfection of a ninja.

The guards on the downstairs tried to come up but they found rains of blades which were coming towards them. They couldn't dodge it.

Rahul was watching all this from behind the sofa. He didn't know who the mysterious person was. He dialed 100 and within few minutes, police came with a large force.

Arjun vanished from the place. When the police arrived the top floor, They found that someone has already done their job.

Rahul came out and he argued to meet the senior most among them. He met the CI of the area and told him all the story. However, the CI didn't believe him and told him that it was all nonsense and he could go to his house.

Rahul couldn't believe his eyes what he had seen. For a moment, he thought that he was watching an action movie. He then remembered about the shadow which he saw previous night.

Rahul walked towards his house, still shocked. He had seen ninjas only in movies and cartoons but never encountered any in real life.

When he reached home, directly he lied on his bed without even changing the clothes. He was thinking about the previous night, "The shadow sort of thing which I had seen yesterday night. I think it was this person only. Who was he? From where did he came from? What's his nationality? Or everything is just fiction, a silly nonsense to prank me. But no, he killed all the gangsters. This is not a prank. Something is serious. I have to find out."

The next day Rahul reached late to his classroom than his usual time. Everyone was already there, chatting about something. He joined them.

"Yes yes, the police had really done a good job", said a voice among the group.

Arjun saw Rahul, his eyes were dull. He asked him, "Hey, you didn't sleep at night? Your eyes are looking red."

Rahul replied with a sleepy sort of voice, "Yes, I didn't sleep yesterday. I was doing an important work which failed."

"Anyway did you see the news today, the police had arrested a big gang of drug dealers yesterday night. They even encountered few of them including their boss. This is a big achievement", said Arjun.

Arjun wanted Rahul to tell something about them so that he could know more.

Rahul's eyes at once turned normal from red when he heard that news from Arjun. He wondered that the police had not mentioned him during the fight, since his friends are not looking at him seriously.

During the end of the college hours, when Rahul was going out alone, Arjun placed his arm on his shoulder and said, "Don't do these type of things again. It is not good. Be normal like us."

Saying this he went away to his destination. Rahul wondered how did he knew about the incident of previous night.

His brain was full of questions and thoughts which didn't have any answers right now. His eyes were turning more red. However, he decided not to do such things again.

On the other hand, Arjun was celebrating his first victory alone in his room. He was now known among the police, though as a wanted but it was okay.

Now, he was thinking about assassinating the master mind behind the drug dealers. He thought of preparing a well plan for his mission.

For two days, he was creating a map for his work plan. He took even the smallest things under consideration.

When he finished his work, he named the mission as 'Mission blind'. Why Blind?

He would deal every single task with secrecy, not even telling the police. He wanted everyone to be blind during the mission.

For everyone to be blind, he has to deal with his tasks at the darkest hours of night when even the moon wouldn't be able to find him.

During the first night, Arjun started moving towards the old spot where he had destroyed the gangsters. When he reached there, he found that the place is guarded by some police.

He couldn't enter them without knocking and he has no right to attack them without any reason. That's why he left that place.

When Arjun was leaving, he noticed two black vans were going one after another as if they are guarding one of them.

He wondered why would two vans roam on the streets at night and like one after another.

Arjun thought something was wrong. He started following them to know where they were going.

After running behind them, he saw the vans entering a house. The house was on the first floor and on the ground floor, there was a garage.

He noticed the shutter of the garage was a little open from the ground. He at once understood something illegal was going inside there.

He heard the door of the van opened and from inside few people wearing black jackets and masks came out.

After that the shutter of the garage opened and few people wearing the same clothes came out. They looked here and there and then talked.

Arjun was unable to listen them since he was watching them from a very far distance. He wondered what sort of things they were doing.

After some time, they again opened the van door and then the scene angered Arjun.

He saw two children were kidnapped and they were tied by rope. He then thought that they must have kept more children like them inside the garage. He became furious and thought of slicing them with his katana.

Though, he didn't do it since he couldn't lose his patience for his temper. He thought of making a strategy. If he directly goes inside then they might harm the children.

He couldn't let them hurt the children.

He found a idea that he could attack the first floor first so that there would be no backup left for defense.

He went near the vans, they were empty. He then ensured that there was no one outside the house.

Then, he went up on the roof from where he could listen the people who were there in the first floor.

He heard voices of some of them, "Did anybody see you coming from that road?"

"No, the whole road was empty. Even the police was not there for patrolling today. They thought they have already arrested the criminals. Ha ha ha ha!"

Arjun even heard sounds of television and snoring. He thought, "Few people are sleeping. The awake ones are those who came just now. It is a good time. Lets do it."

And then, there was a sound of the window glass breaking into pieces. The kidnappers inside didn't know what happened and before that only they found blades coming towards them.

The sleeping fellows woke up and they tried to hide their faces with the pillows. But they couldn't do it since they were sent to hell before that.

Arjun took out his katana and slashed each and every person on the first floor. He didn't show mercy on a single person. He made them cried and then destroyed them.

The kidnappers on the ground floor heard the footsteps coming from the first floor. They thought they should check once what had been happening.

When they went upstairs, the scene frightened them. Everyone was lying dead and in the middle of the room, Arjun was standing with the bloody katana in his hand.

They tried to flee but found their legs hit by some blades. After then, they were unable to see each other's face again.

Arjun went downstairs and opened the garage. He found two persons standing with a cricket bat. He slashed them with his katana but didn't kill them. He left them alive for the police to arrest them and take the credit.

The children were watching everything from behind. They thought a super hero was assigned to take them back home.

Arjun freed them and then asked one of them to dial 100. Within few minutes police came to the area. Arjun had already escaped from that place before any one came there.

Again, the police found their work done by someone else. It was the same CI who was there in the drug dealer case. His reaction after seeing all this was unbelievable.

He asked the children, "Who has saved you from them?"

They all replied, "A super hero came who was looking like a ninja wearing a mask."

The CI was now doubtful. The same story which he had heard from the boy during the drug case.

He even asked one of the kidnappers who were left alive, they also narrated the same story.

The CI now understood that someone is there who is trained and maybe he is helping now but later he could even go against them.

Therefore, he decided not to release this news to the media. He even told the children to keep it a secret.

The CI wanted to tell this news to the commissioner of police. This maybe dangerous in the future if the police couldn't do anything due to a mysterious man. This step was a problem for Arjun and his mission blind.

Arjun's plan for revealing his look might be a problem for him. He may choose his time strategy wisely to avoid getting caught.

The next day during the college hours, again it was a talk about the previous day's news. This time Arjun didn't talk much as he knew while talking he may spit out everything and this would create a problem.

During that night, Arjun went out for his mission. However, he couldn't explore much since the police had increased the patrolling.

He had to hide many times since the police were frequently making rounds. He couldn't even leave the roof tops due to them. Though, he found some clues about the drug dealers by searching the first battle place, the building.

When he came back home, he analyzed a small copy of a bill of a medicine shop.

He thought in his mind, "The name written is Aryan Malhotra. Who is this person? Maybe the shop owner, or someone else. But he is the clue for all this. This bill might be attached to a cardboard box. I can see the address. 122 Manav colony, street no 23. Manav colony! Wait! I think I know this place. This place was abandoned few years ago. It was only allowed for business purpose since it had a warehouse. Maybe, that warehouse is the key to my mission. I will go there tomorrow. And also to that medicine shop."

Tomorrow morning, Arjun went to that medicine shop. It was a holiday in his college. He carried a small knife with him, in case of emergency.

Arjun arrived in front of the medical shop. The owner was sitting there. He was not very old and not very young either.

Arjun called him, "Excuse me!"

The person got attention. He stood up and came near to him.

Arjun continued in an informal tone, "Aryan Malhotra sent me to collect the materials. Maybe he had made the payment, if not he would do it soon. Allow me to take the materials."

The man looked here and there to ensure it no one was watching him. He then took out a small package and gave it to Arjun.

His doubt was correct. He took the package

From him and started walking as fast as possible towards his house.

When he came back home, he opened the package. As he as expected, it contained false medicines. He thought of complaining the police as he had received false medicines from that shop.

Arjun even requested them not to reveal his identity otherwise his life would be at danger.

The police accepted his request and asked him to give the address and go home. He did as they said.

The police at once charged for the medical shop. When they reached there, they found the information correct. The shop owner was arrested and Arjun was now thinking of his next step.

On the same night, he explored the city once again. He went to the seized medical shop to collect some more clues but he found few people were standing behind the shop.

They were carrying guns and other sharp weapons. Arjun at once understood that they have come to erase all the clues.

Without wasting any time, he attacked them with his katana. He slashed each and every person standing there. However, during the struggle, someone from them fired a bullet. Though it didn't hit Arjun but the sound of the gun shot reached the police.

He quickly strike the leftovers and took whatever he felt like important. Without wasting a second, he escaped before the police arrived.

He came back home fast and quickly took out whatever he has got. He started analyzing them one by one.

However, nothing of them seemed to be important. He was frustrated and threw them to the dustbin near.

Nevertheless, he found an envelope which went out of the window after it came out of the paper cover. Arjun tried to snatch it before it falls but it went out.

He leaned from the window to see if anybody was there who could help. He found a young girl was walking with a trolley and a bag pack. It seemed like she was a newly joined student in first year and was going to her room with the essentials.

Arjun shouted from the window, "Hello! Excuse me! Could you listen to me?"

The girl looked here and there to see if anyone was calling her. She was unable to find and even she wondered who would call her at midnight.

Arjun continued, "Over here. I'm here. Look upward."

She looked upward to see a boy was calling her from his room. She called out, "What do you want? Why are you calling me like that? I will complain to the principal."

Arjun thought she had misunderstood him. He quickly called, "No, actually an envelope has fallen just now from the window. It is very important. Could you please bring it to me here. I will be grateful."

She searched here and there and found a peach coloured envelop. She took it in her hands and started going upstairs.

Arjun quickly hide his suit and other things and opened a book on the study table so that the girl didn't doubt him.

She knocked the door of room no eight. Arjun opened the door and he found the girl carrying the envelope.

She said, "Here's your envelope. I am sorry for my rude behavior. I am new to this place and didn't know anyone. That's why I felt insecure."

Arjun took the envelope, "Thank you very much. This is very important. It accidently went out of the window. I will be grateful to you."

"Most welcome", she replied. "What's your good name?"

He smiled at her and said, "I'm Arjun. First year student from class 1B."

She exclaimed, "1B! Hey we are in the same class. I am Meera kumara. Nice to meet you."

"Nice to meet you too", he replied joyfully.

Arjun continued further, "if you require any help regarding college lectures and notes you can ask me. I'll always there to help you out. Anyway you gave back my envelope."

She asked him curiously, "What it contains? You told something important."

Arjun didn't want her to know the truth. He lied, "Actually this is my old friend's letter. He doesn't have a mobile phone so, he send letters to me every month. His family income is very low. I also write letters to him."

She exclaimed, "Good! Still some people are following the old ways. I know, letters have more feelings than online texts."

"You are right", said Arjun as if he was really agreeing with her.

Meera noticed the time and said, "Okay, I have to go now. Meet you tomorrow in the class hours. Bye for now."

Arjun again smiled at her, "Yeah! Bye. And don't shy to ask to help."

Meera turned back and started to go to her room. Arjun's mind was still lost on her. He wasn't thinking about the important work he had to do but lost in the world of imaginations.

His senses came back when he lost her visual. He then got to know that he was staring at her for a long time.

He thought in his mind, "What happened to me? Why am I doing like this? It never happened before. What kind of feeling is this? Maybe something I don't know. Leave it, let's focus on our work."

He then closed the door and took the envelope in his hands.

He took a deep breath to focus his mind.

Arjun after relaxing himself opened the envelope. He was surprised to find a photo. "What? A photo! What kind of photo is this?"

He looked at it carefully and said, "Oh! I got it. These is a laboratory beaker which is placed on a table. It contained a colourless liquid. Maybe water, or something else. Maybe acetic acid, it is used in medicines. Something will be there. They must have given any information about it. Maybe I had left it in the medical shop during the fight. I have to go there and search again."

Arjun again wore the suit and went out for the second time in this night. He came near the shop but the policemen were standing there to investigate the bodies. Arjun stayed hidden and tried not to make any sound. He focused on his ears and tried to listen what they were saying.

"Sir, this must be a gang war between two groups or a small fight."

The CI was also standing there. He didn't thought it as a gang war. Gang war means rain of bullets and sounds. However, they had just got a sound of single bullet which was fired from here.

He was sure that the shadow sort of thing which did two main jobs in the city must have done it. But he didn't tell anyone about this. He wanted to keep it a secret.

Arjun was listening all this from a hidden place. He thought in his mind, "I have to meet the CI once again but this time as a ninja, not Arjun. I must tell him about the information which I have received. If he could help me then it will be easier for me to handle the mission blind."

He thought of meeting the CI alone in his house. He followed the CI throughout the whole way to his house.

When he reached there he waited till the CI was left alone. He thought of entering the house. He knocked at the door. The CI opened it was shocked to see a person in fancy clothes which looked dangerous though.

Arjun said, "Please don't be scared. I need your help it is very urgent. Please."

"Who are you", asked the CI still surprised?

I am the shadow sort of thing which you were thinking from a long time. My intentions are not bad. I just want your help to solve the case and the drug dealing mission.

The CI took a minute and then he remembered the story of the shadow. He said, "So it was you who is doing all our jobs in the night. Are you an agent or something? Why are you helping us? Come inside, let's sit and talk."

Arjun went inside, the house was a quite luxury one for an ordinary CI. The CI pointed towards the sofa. Arjun sat there with him and started the discussion.

"Sir, actually I am investigating few drug dealers who are hiding inside the city. One night when I was roaming, I saw two black vans. At first I thought it was those drug dealers only but later I found they were kidnappers. Sir, I want you to help me out. If you couldn't then please do not reveal my identity. I am just a protector of the citizens. I am not a criminal."

The CI understood everything. He said, "Alright! I won't reveal your identity. I can only help you by giving the past details of the criminals. Rest you have to do alone. Go ahead. I hate those people who deal with drugs."

Arjun smiled behind the mask and said, "Thank you so much sir. I hope you will cooperate. I would give my mission details to you every week so that you could analyze. I have to leave, bye for now."

The CI stopped him, "Wait gentleman, what's your name?"

"Agnivayu", a voice came from behind the mask.

The CI allowed him to go.

The next day, Arjun prepared of spending the night not for his duty.

He arrived in his classroom and found someone whom he thought he had met before. It was Meera.

She saw him and even raised her hand but Arjun didn't recognize her. She came near him and asked, "Hi, what's going on? Your eyes are red, didn't you sleep at night?"

Arjun at once remembered the envelope incident and he finally retained her name, "Oh Meera! Sorry, I forgot your name. Please don't mind."

She was astonished, "What! You forgot my name. Wow! I think you studied a lot yesterday."

"Maybe, sorry for that" replied Arjun with tightness.

Meera saw sweat coming out on her forehead. She patted her head and said, "Hey chill. Why are you feeling so discomfort? I was just joking."

They both talked with each other for a very long time even after the college hours.

Arjun had completely forgot his tasks while talking with Meera. He was completely lost in his world.

That night Arjun didn't go out for exploration. He thought in his mind while lying awake on the bed, "Should I tell everyone about the powers and the suit? No, they can urge me to misuse them or even for their personal tasks. I won't."

Arjun thought that he would never tell anyone until it is emergency. However, he would at least appear in front of them in that suit so they may discuss about the shadows with each other.

Basically, he wanted to be famous in front of his friends. Though not as Arjun, but as Agnivayu. For this, he was lucky enough to get a good opportunity. Though it was not good for his friends.

During the end college hours when everyone was going back to their homes or rooms, Arjun was with his friends heading towards the hostel.

One of his friends, Ishita stayed nearby in a two-storey house. She was the local person of the city. She lived with her family in that house. It was a nuclear family.

When Ishita reached the college main gate, she was kidnapped and taken away by a black van. The other students who were coming behind her screamed very loudly, "A student is kidnapped here openly!"

Arjun was about to enter the hostel but he stepped back after hearing the screams. He turned around to find a black van in which Ishita was kidnapped.

He quickly entered in his room, changed the clothes and got ready to rescue her. However, he couldn't go through the main gate since it was evening time and still the sun is above head.

He didn't want anybody to see him. But he had to rescue his friend at any cost otherwise they may harm her. He thought of something else.

Arjun remembered a small gate which always remained closed since many years. He carefully reached the rooftop of the hostel building through his window and went to the small gate.

No one noticed a black shadow running on the rooftops even in the evening light. He reached the gate, still closed.

He jumped over it and reached the other side of the wall. Now he could chase the van. The possible location and routes of the van was running in his mind.

He followed his mind and luckily, it was correct. He found the van running in the west direction.

He started chasing it till it's location.

The location was a warehouse which was covered with factories besides. There were several kidnappers who were staying there.

Arjun saw the vehicle went inside. He peeked from a transparent glass cover which was attached on the rooftop.

Ishita was thrown outside from the vehicle by the person. After that four people came out of it.

Ishita saw her rival Muskan standing in front of her. Muskan's father was standing next to her, fully guarded by gangsters with rifles in their hands.

The whole place was a business property of her father. He was known for his power and never get caught for any illegal activities.

Ishita's hands were tied and she was kneeling in front of them. She asked, "Why did you do this? What did I do?"

Muskan got angry, "Yes yes, What did you do! Don't you remember you complained about me to the principal. He scolded me because of you and you are telling why I did this."

Ishita raised her voice, "I complained because you bully the juniors a lot just for your entertainment. You are wrong that's why I did this."

"I can do anything, you don't have any right to complain", shouted Muskan. She continued, "You can try your best but you can never escape from this place. You see, I will ruin your family. My father is the king of this place."

At that instant, a sound came like a glass was broken. Muskan and her father was stunned when they saw a mysterious person standing behind Ishita.

Her father said, "Hey you! How did you enter my property without my permission. Get lost."

Arjun replied in a casual voice, "Same thing I am here to tell you. Leave her alone and get lost from this place. Otherwise you all will never see each other again."

Muskan's father became angry. He shouted, "I will kill you. You think that wearing a dress like that and carrying a false sword will afraid us? You are wrong. This is not a fancy dress competition mister, go away otherwise my guards will not leave you alive."

Arjun smiled and said in a relaxing tone, "Sir, I challenge you! Send any one of your person to have a duel with me. If I lose, I will go. But, If I won, You have to leave my friend and get lost from this place. Do you accept?"

Before her father could say anything, one of the guards came running towards Arjun, carrying a large knife.

Arjun took a standoff and when the guard came near, he strike him to hell. The other people who were standing next to Ishita took a step back after they saw the incident.

Arjun kept the kanto inside and took out the shining katana which was tied in his back. The shine of the metal represented his Aura. He said, "I am Agnivayu, ready to slash you all."

The boss ordered, "Guards! Kill him."

Arjun saw the men were heading towards him from all directions. He was surrounded by a large group. A group of about fifty to sixty men.

He took out his kunai's and threw them behind. The guards fell down as the blades hit them. The back area was busy while dealing with the blades. Many people fell over one another instead of dodging them.

Arjun threw the shurikens towards the guards carrying rifles. His aim was like Arjuna of Mahabharata. Every blade hit the correct target.

Muskan and her father was watching all this from behind. Their hands shivered from fear. Ishita was watching all this from behind.

Arjun was showing no mercy to any of the guards. His beast mode was on and he was just slashing his rivals.

Not even a single rival blade could touch him. He destroyed them with his katana.

Ishita wondered who he was. She had seen these type of persons in movies. However, she had never thought in her life that she would experience it once through her eyes.

After sending everyone to hell, Arjun came face to face with Muskan's father. He said, "This is my power. Your daughter did many wrong things but no one could ever complain. If one is doing it you are kidnapping. I am leaving you now so that you could overcome your mistake. This should never happen again. Get lost!"

They both hurried out from that place.

Ishita was tied in a place. Arjun went there and freed her. He was about to leave but he thought to staying with her to give her protection.

Ishita admired her, "Thank you so much for saving me. I will be really grateful to you."

"Most welcome! It is my job" said Arjun.

Ishita wanted to know who he was, such strong and powerful man. "Who are you? Where did you came from? What name did you tell that time, I didn't hear it properly?"

"I am Agnivayu" replied Arjun. "I am an Indian only. I had received special powers from my parents."

"Wow!" replied Ishita. "You are so lucky. Could I meet your parents once, I would love to."

Arjun had tears in his eyes but he didn't showed her. He said in a calm voice, "Unfortunately, they are not in this world anymore. I had lost them in an accident. After that only I received these powers when my father came to my dream once."

Ishita at once remembered Arjun's incident. Arjun also remembered that at once. However, both have different feelings.

Ishita asked him, "I am sorry to hear that. 'Agnivayu' is your real name? Or what is your real name? Please share, I won't tell anyone."

Arjun looked very worried that time.

Nevertheless, he decided to tell Ishita about the truth. He said to Ishita, "This is my humble request. Please don't tell anyone about this until emergency. I am on a mission. Promise me you will not do that."

Ishita held his hands and said, "I promise. You can do your tasks freely." She was excited to hear the name but she didn't know the surprise.

Arjun took a deep breath and said, "I am Arjun Yadav, your college friend." After that he removed his mask.

The ground slipped beneath Ishita's feet. Never she had a surprise like that in her life.

She jumped on him and gave him a tight hug. She still couldn't believe the ninja was her friend.

After the excitement, Arjun said, "Ishita please don't share this with anyone. You have promised me until it is emergency."

Ishita smiled happily and answered, "Don't worry, you can trust your friend. But any time if I shall be in trouble, You will have to protect me."

Arjun sighed a relief, "Yes, always. You just need to call Agnivayu in a loud voice, it will reach my brain and I will be there to help you. But use it only when you are in serious trouble, not for playtime."

Ishita agreed and they both went back towards their home. Arjun guarded her from rooftops till she reached her house safely.

Arjun went to his hostel after that, tired.

He lied on the bed and thought, "The whole day went very busily today.

Oh! I forgot something. I should tell the CI about this incident of kidnapping. I will tell him tomorrow. I am very tired now. Tomorrow night I shall go to his house and give him the information."

He was very tired that night so he slept quickly without wondering about the burdens.

The next day was a public holiday in the city. Their college was also closed that day.

Arjun woke up late but he managed to get ready for the day without any delay.

He came before the window to enjoy the view.

He saw many of his friends were playing cricket. He decided to join them.

He played cricket for almost two hours and then he realized that he had to meet the CI and also research about the dealers.

He went back to his room to find a parcel has came for him. He quickly took it inside and shut the door.

He opened the package to find a bar code reader which he had ordered to see the old package which he had taken from the medical shop.

When he scanned the code, his happiness knew no bounds. He finally received an address from the code which could be the final destination.

However, when he read the address he stood still for a moment. The same address which he had went yesterday. The same location, the same warehouse. Overall, the same property.

He realized, "Muskan's father. The drug mafia's mastermind. If I had known this earlier, I must not have left him alive."

He banged the desk with the anger and regret. First time, he had been looking so frustrated.

However, he thought of calling Ishita once. He dialed, "Hello Ishita, I want to know a very urgent information."

From the other side, Ishita replied, "Yes, yes. Tell me? It looks like you want to talk something important."

"Could you tell me the name of Muskan's father", said Arjun with a regretful voice?

"Md Yusuf", replied Ishita.

Arjun acknowledged her and cut the call. He was literally in a hurry to know about the mastermind.

He opened the chrome and searched about Md Yusuf. He found the one whom he was searching for. He was described as a pillar of business in local places.

He shouted in his mind, "You are not a pillar, you are the destroyer. But this time, you will be destroyed."

He waited till midnight to meet the CI.

During the darkest hours, he went to the CI's house with the information.

He discussed with the CI about the information, told him everything about the mastermind and even explained the incident of the fight.

The CI said, "Great job Agnivayu. I will send all this information to the higher authorities."

Arjun at once stopped him, "No sir. He is a very powerful businessman. He can escape anytime. The only way to stop him is by sending him to hell."

The CI didn't felt it good but still he agreed with the hero since his argument was not wrong. He was saying right.

However, The CI told him not to go outside for exploration for few days. He wanted Md Yusuf to ensure that Agnivayu is not in the city anymore.

He accepted this and was ready to deal with his mission. The breakthrough was online.

The next day, he started to live like a normal student just which was temporary. He did all assignments, projects, notes and class works.

However, he couldn't find Meera for till the whole day. He was thinking in his mind about the different feelings he had for her. He was honest from his heart and his feelings were not meant for any bad intentions.

He was wondering about their first meeting which was quite unexpected.

He spent a whole week like a normal student. He was missing his suit and the beautiful exploration which he could again experience anytime but he didn't do anything for mission blind. Though, mission blind was known to two of his people and it didn't remained blind anymore.

However, for one thing he was troubled during the college hours and even during the holidays was missing of Meera.

He asked few people whether she had changed the college, batch or anything but everyone told him that she was missingfor quite few days without any message or information.

They were thinking that she had left the college as she didn't want to study anymore.

Arjun felt every argument nonsense. He thought in his mind, "Meera is a very good student. She like studies more than anyone else. Then how could someone say that she left due to not interest in academics? Something is wrong. Really, she is missing from a different point of view."

He was wondering all this, sitting on a bench near the college garden. At the same time, Muskan arrived with a regret on her face.

At first Arjun thought that she must have known everything, but later he sighed a relief as she said, "Arjun I am sorry, I was not aware of what might happen. You must have heard that Ishita was kidnapped few days ago. Actually, I did this with my father. However, I leaft her peacefully and later, realized my mistake."

"So it was you who did that", Arjun tried to act in front on her.

Muskan replied, "Yes it was me. But now I realized my mistake and I would never do it. Even I apologized to Ishita. She only told me to narrate the same here."

Arjun thought that she was telling the truth. Her expression of regret was natural. He said, "It's okay if you realized your mistake. Don't do it next time. Let's be friends."

They both shake their hands and after that Muskan went back to her work.

Arjun was unable to predict what would happen next. However, he decided destiny to continue his journey further.

Nevertheless, Arjun got a very good idea. He could use Muskan's help to find out information about Md Yusuf.

But he didn't want to use her like a pawn to defeat the king. He didn't want to break someone's heart.

However, for the protection of the youth of city, he has defeat those drug dealers. Instead of one good friend, he has to save the crowd.

The destiny is playing a game with him right now. Even after becoming a super human, he was unable to win with destiny. Though, he was given two choices.

He wasn't looking good. Meera was missing, destiny's game. Life was looking unreal.

That night, he wore his suit after a long time and went to meet the CI.

He knocked the door, the CI took a step backward when he saw the warrior.

Arjun said, "I want to discuss very important things. Please let me in."

The CI allowed him to ask anything.

Arjun told him about the missing case of Meera and about his next plan.

The CI said the final words to him, "Do what your heart is saying to you, but don't forget that you had a friend who tried his best to serve you. Go ahead Agnivayu."

Arjun was motivated through his words. He decided to work on his plan.

He met Muskan daily and increased his relations with her. He even told her that Meera had been missing since long time and her phone was even switched off.

Her room was locked. It seemed to him that her goods and items were still there inside which were covered with dust.

He was missing her from long time. Their bond had become very close since a long time. Every day they used to share their thoughts and help each other.

Now without her, Arjun's life was not going as smooth as earlier.

However, to find her he has to first accomplish his mission. 'Mission blind' was very important for the recovery of the city.

Maybe he could find her later. He wished she might not be in danger. But who knows the actual reality? No one among them.

Arjun's plan was going well. He had been acquiring details about Md Yusuf through her daughter.

One day, Muskan called Arjun to have a nice talk with her father after her father's permission.

Arjun wondered, "He knows Agnivayu, not Arjun. I must go there. Maybe, I could know his reality or about him only. He looks like a typical gangster businessman.

It was a nice Sunday. The house, sorry! The mansion of Md Yusuf was shining like a large diamond is built on the earth.

From inside, it looked like a five-star hotel. The staffs were running here and there for the welcome of Arjun.

The scene could confuse anyone if it was a private property or something unimaginable.

Muskan greeted Arjun and requested him to come inside. Her few more friends had also come.

He went inside an sat on a comfy sofa. He was feeling like sleeping on that, no tensions, nothing all who could disturb him. However, he controlled his emotions once he remembered about 'Mission Blind'.

Arjun had a nice talk with few of the friends. He was even thinking in his mind, "All this, the mansion, the cars, the luxury furniture, this cozy sofa has come at the cost of many lives which you have taken Md Yusuf. I will pay for it. Just wait for sometime."

After few minutes, Md Yusuf arrived from the starirs. He was wearing his favorite navy blue suit, a luxury wrist watch on his right hand and his expensive leather black shoes. All at the cost of innocent people.

Arjun's mind was full with anger and frustration. He wanted to kill him right now with the fruit knife placed on the dining table.

However, he controlled himself again. He was doing this since long time, waiting game.

Yusuf saw Arjun was standing to greet him. He was looking smart, wearing a blue jacket and black cargo pants.

Yusuf smiled at him and said, "Welcome to my palace dear! Consider this your own house only. Don't shy to place or use anything."

Arjun smiled the honest one and said, "Sorry, but I can't consider it to be my palace. I want to gain everything by my hard work and dedication with honesty. That will give me more satisfaction and confidence."

Yusuf expressed, "I am impressed with your words Arjun. Good thought."

"Please never mind my words. I don't want to make you angry" muttered Arjun.

"No my boy, never" said Yusuf. He then added, "Come, I will show you my office."

Arjun agreed and they both went to the office building through a luxury car. The building was few steps from the mansion.

Arjun entered the office, there were guards every where his eyes went. They were carrying arms in their hands. Their eyes were covered with black glasses and wore a black suit which looked very premium.

The office building was as luxury as the mansion. Yusuf took Arjun to his seat where he used to control his entire business.

For a moment, Arjun wondered why he was allowing him to see all this.

He stood still for a moment when he heard a sound. It looked like a girl was calling someone.

His hearing ability was very good. He at once understood that someone is captured inside the room from which sound was coming.

However, he didn't ask Yusuf about all this.

Yusuf was showing him all his works and plans. Arjun asked a different question to him, "Sir, how many body guards do you have? I am just seeing them till I entered. They are every where."

Yusuf replied, "Approx five-hundred. But wait, why are you asking that?"

"Just asking casually" said Arjun.

He decided to save the girl whom Yusuf had captured. He waited till night for this moment.

Nevertheless, this time he decided to end the game and the mission blind. He was determined to attack from the front.

He wore his suit, draw his blades and was fully prepared for the battle. Before going out, he honored his katana by touching his forehead with the blade and then took it behind.

After doing a small time meditation, he started to walk to the place.

However, a surprise was waiting for him near the office, he had never thought of.

What was the surprise? Readers, don't guess.

When he stepped his foot just before entering the office, he was shocked to see Yusuf, standing there with his guards.

He laughed his devil style and said, "Agnivayu! Arjun! You thought I am a fool right. I know you since the first meeting. When you were telling your friend about the reality, I was there listening your every word. This was all my plan and now you can't do anything. I will kill you right here."

"Oh! So finally you did that thing. I already doubted you when you were showing me about your plans and even your rooms today. I have come to rescue the girl whom you have captured. If anyone comes in my way, I will sent him to hell. I think you had forgot the first fight. That's why you want to challenge me."

"Yes, I don't remember defeats as I only like to win" said Yusuf.

He added, "Don't you know who that girl is?"

"Tell me now" ordered Arjun.

Yusuf paused for a moment and said with a bold expression, "Meera, your bond."

Arjun became angry, "Yusuf! Just leave her. Otherwise you will not see tomorrow's sun."

Yusuf laughed again and shouted, "Oh really! Then fight my bodyguards. I have imported them specially for you. They are very skilled. They are warriors who will show you the power of me. Now you will understand, Yusuf is a bad man. Go ahead guards, kill him."

He went inside his office to hide. The guards surrounded Arjun from all sides.

Arjun took the standoff to declare the battle.

He strike each and everyone with his katana. Few more were coming from inside. He threw his blades and the guards fell on one another when it hit them.

He took out each and every person showing no mercy. He was very angry due to Meera's captive.

He finally took down all guards outside the building. When he entered inside, he saw a blade coming towards him. He dodged it showing reflexes. However, he was shocked to see the front scene. Four people just looking like him carrying katana were standing in front.

He accepted the challenge. He said to himself, "This would be tough, but more fun. Come on guys, I am waiting."

The fight started and Arjun was now facing a better difficulty than previous. He had to make extra effort to hit them. He had to use all his skills which was given to him for the defense of humanity.

However, when he was still unable to down anyone, he became angry.

That anger turned on his ghost mode. After that he sent each person to hell. But he even got injured and some of his powers reduced.

Then also, he managed to fight the rest of the people just for Meera.

He opened another hall door and found more guards. He killed them one by one but got more injured.

However, the injury didn't make him weak. A wounded lion is more dangerous than a normal one.

He then entered the final stage to find only Yusuf pointing a gun towards Meera. Her hands were tied with rope.

Yusuf said, "If you dare to step forward, I will kill her. Your mission would pass but you will lose your best friend."

Arjun stood still just opposite to Yusuf. Meera was at gun point. He didn't want any disaster to happen that time.

Though, he said to Yusuf, "Meera is not just my best friend. She is my life. I can do anything for her. You want to see."

Arjun took a deep breath, stepped a little backward and directly jumped towards him with his katana.

Yusuf fired a bullet on him. It hit his chest. But before that, just a moment of seconds, he destroyed him with his katana.

However, due to that bullet Arjun fell down. Meera came towards him. He was still having sense. He cut her tied rope and told her to call the police.

Meera took Yusuf's phone, who had already died, and dialed 100.

Arjun closed him eyes. Meera didn't knew earlier that the warrior is Arjun. Her eyes were filled with tears.

Within few minutes, the CI arrived with the police force. The ambulance also arrived as the CI knew what might had happened.

Arjun was taken to the ICU. The doctors were shocked when they saw Arjun's heart beat stopped once but after sometime, it again started, like a normal person.

Arjun woke up. He understood everything and thanked his father.

Readers, Arjun has lost his powers and this was now his second life.

He opened the ICU door to find Meera waiting for him outside. She hugged him, tears in her eyes.

The CI now came to know about the real name of the warrior. He gave Arjun a salute. The whole police force followed their CI.

Arjun and Meera later completed their studies and started their new life together.

Arjun's feelings, "Finally, I have you. I promise not to leave you alone and always help you."

Meera smiled at her, "Same to you. You will always remain a hero for me even if you don't have any powers."

The sunset looked like the end of the past whether it is good or bad and continue a new day just like a new life.

However, Arjun's katana stayed with him forever, not leaving the hero and giving him the honor, he deserve to get.

THE END

About the Author

Ankan Sarkar dreams to become the next generation author where he wants to make the people realize about the importance of life which has become just a profit or loss statement. The importance of books and persons meant everything for him.

His books will make readers to ensure the importance of these values which are lost among the present youth.

The most important thing about his books are that it values human and feelings more than something else.

"Some Choices can be done together.
Just work hard to Achieve them."

__Ankan Sarkar

Words of Acknowledgement
from the Author

This book is completed on the occasion of Father's Day. My father had always supported me throughout my life and I know that he will do more for me to succeed.

My mother even played an important role in my life. She didn't left any stone unturned to see me successful. I am still a child but I promise not to let anyone feel regret.

This book is also for someone special which I never wanted to tell the readers till they could find it.

Thank you dear parents to support me. I can't repay for what you have done for me.

Message for Readers

Thank you so much to the readers to read this book till the end.

I am very grateful if you liked my story.

I promise not to let anyone down.

9 798899 847974